I can build a house!

Story by Shigeo Watanabe
Pictures by Yasuo Ohtomo

CREATIVE PLAY

PHILOMEL BOOKS

Text © 1982 by Shigeo Watanabe • Illustrations © 1982 by Yasuo Ohtomo • American text © 1983 by Philomel Books • All rights reserved
Published in the United States by Philomel Books, a division of The Putnam Publishing Group, 51 Madison Avenue, New York, NY 10010
Originally published by Fukuinkan Shoten, Tokyo, 1982 • Library of Congress CIP information at back of book • Printed in U.S.A.

There! I did it.

Uh, oh!

I think I'll make a
bigger house this time.

Up it goes!

There! I did it.

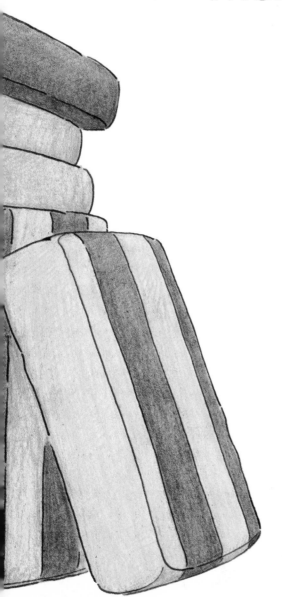

Oh, no!

I know what to use!

Shall I put it this way?

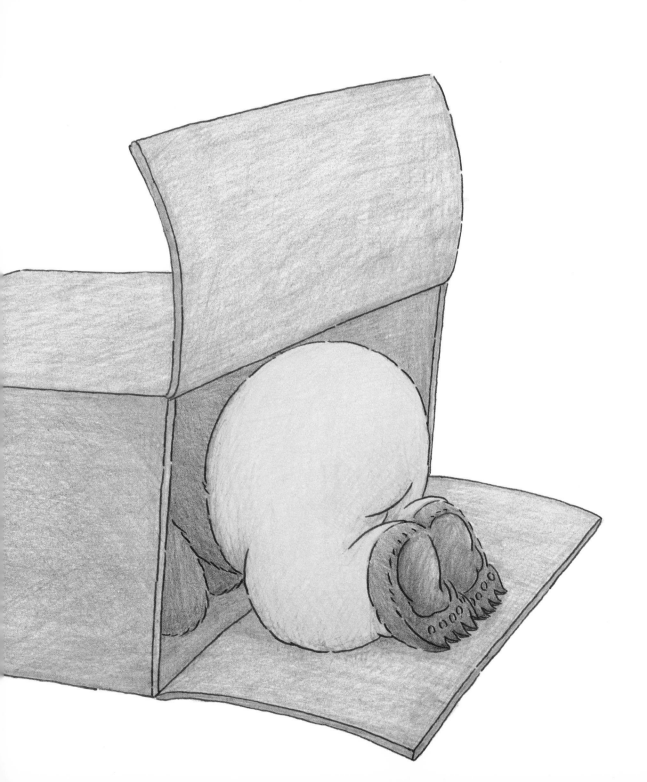

Or maybe this way?

How about this way?

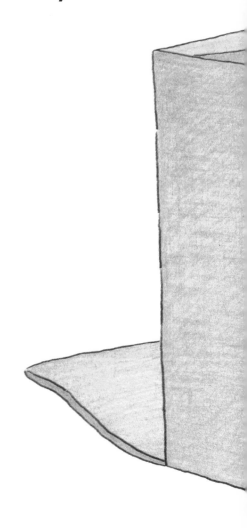

Now I've got it.

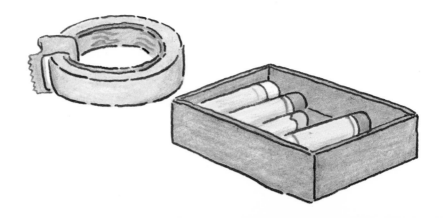

I did it all by myself!

Library of Congress Cataloging in Publication Data
Watanabe, Shigeo, 1928–
I can build a house!
(An I can do it all by myself book; 7)
Translation of: Boku ouchi o tsukurunda!
Summary: Bear perseveres until he finds just the
right material for building the perfect house.
[1. Dwellings—Fiction. 2. Building materials—
Fiction] I. Ohtomo, Yasuo, ill.   II. Title.
PZ7.W2615Iac   1983   [E]   82–22386
ISBN 0–399–20950–6